# Richard Scarry's
## Busy Day Storybooks

# Sergeant Murphy's Busy Day

J.B. COMMUNICATIONS INC.

Well before the sun is up, Sergeant Murphy's telephone rings. "DRRINNNG!!!" Sergeant Murphy wakes up. "Hello?" he answers the telephone, "Sergeant Murphy here." It is Deputy Flo calling from the police station.

"I have looked everywhere, Sergeant Murphy," she says, "but I can't find your whistle! You can't work today without it!"

"Don't worry, Flo," answers Sergeant Murphy. "My whistle is right here beside me. Thanks for calling!"

The Murphy family gets up for another busy day.

While Mrs. Patsy Murphy dresses little Bridget, Sergeant Murphy prepares breakfast.

Umm! Don't those eggs and bacon smell good?

Soon it is time for Sergeant Murphy and Bridget to go.

"Goodbye!"

Sergeant Murphy drives Bridget to the
kindergarten in his motorcycle's sidecar.

On the way, his motorcycle telephone begins to ring.
"DRRINNNG! DRRINNNG!"

It's Mrs. Murphy on the line.

"Sarge, you left your whistle behind this morning, but don't worry, I will leave it at the police station."

Sergeant Murphy
drops Bridget off at
kindergarten.
"Bye, Daddy!" calls
Bridget, as she enters.
"Goodbye, Bridget!
Have fun!" calls
Sergeant Murphy.

"DRRINNNG!" goes Sergeant
Murphy's telephone.
It's Mayor Fox calling.
"Sergeant Murphy, there is a
giant traffic jam outside.
Busytown needs your help to
clear it up!"

"Yes sir, Mayor Fox!"
replies Sergeant
Murphy. "I'm on my
way!"

8

But Sergeant Murphy wonders how he will direct traffic without his whistle.

Just then, he sees a band playing in the park. He stops and asks if he may borrow the cymbals.

With the cymbals tucked neatly in his sidecar, he speeds away.

9

My, what a traffic jam!
"Just stay calm, everybody!" Sergeant Murphy says.

"Clang!" Sergeant Murphy directs cars to the left. "Clang!" he directs cars to the right. The traffic jam is sorted out.

Good work!

Directing traffic makes Sergeant Murphy hungry.
He stops for a donut and hot chocolate at Humperdink's
bakery.

His telephone rings.

"DRRINNNG! DRRINNNG!" It's Deputy Flo, calling from
the police station.

"Mrs. Murphy has
brought your
whistle!" says Flo.

"Thank you, Flo!"
answers Sergeant
Murphy. "I'll be over
soon to fetch it."

But before he can
finish his donut, his
telephone rings again!

Why, it's little Sophie Pig. She is crying! While she was shopping with her mother at the supermarket, she got lost.

"Don't worry, Sophie!" says Sergeant Murphy.
"I'm on my way!"
Before you can say "hot chocolate," he's off!

VRROOOM!

On the way, Sergeant Murphy's telephone rings again! It's Sophie's mother on the line. She, too, is crying! She can't find her daughter anywhere in the supermarket!

"Just stay calm!" Sergeant Murphy says. "I will find her for you."

At the supermarket, Sergeant Murphy finds Sophie and brings her to her mother. Thank goodness for Sergeant Murphy!

Sergeant
Murphy
looks at
his watch.
It's time
to give a
traffic-safety
lesson at
school!

"DRRINNNG!" sounds Sergeant Murphy's telephone.
It's Deputy Flo again.
"Sergeant Murphy, since you didn't come for your whistle,
I'm leaving it at Humperdink's bakery."
"Thank you, Flo," says Sergeant Murphy.

15

On his way to school, Sergeant Murphy wonders how he will instruct the children without his whistle. But he gets an idea and borrows Huckle's bicycle bell.

"Ring! Ring! Stop!" directs Sergeant Murphy. "Ring! Ring! GO!"

That's a pretty funny police whistle, Sergeant Murphy!

It is time for Sergeant Murphy to coach the school's soccer team.

Without his whistle to coach the team, Sergeant Murphy borrows a school band tuba.
Huckle kicks the soccer ball high in the sky, but no one sees it come down again.

"That ball went out of bounds!" says Sergeant Murphy.
He tries to blow the tuba, but no sound comes out.
He blows harder...

17

"TOOOOT!" sounds the tuba, as the soccer ball flies out.

"That sure is the funniest coaching whistle I've ever seen!" laughs Huckle.

"But it works!" answers Sergeant Murphy, "TOOOOT!!!"

After soccer practice, Sergeant Murphy drives to pick up Bridget at the kindergarten.

"Hi, Daddy!" she waves. "Have you had a busy day?"

"Oh, yes," replies Sergeant Murphy, "and my busy day is not yet finished!"
Sergeant Murphy drives with Bridget to Humperdink's bakery to pick up his whistle.

Able Baker Charlie
is there to greet them.

"I'm sorry, Sergeant
Murphy," Charlie says,
"Baker Humperdink just
left, and he took your
whistle with him!"
Poor Sergeant Murphy.

Just then, the telephone rings.

20

"It's for you!" says Charlie,
handing Sergeant Murphy the telephone.

It's Mrs. Murphy.

"Could you come
home soon, please,
Sarge? It's important!"
"Okay, Patsy!" he
replies. "We're on
our way home!"

What a surprise! Baker Humperdink, Sophie, Sophie's mother, Flo, and even Able Baker Charlie are there. Baker Humperdink hands Sergeant Murphy his whistle. "Thank you for having found our little Sophie today! I've baked you this whistle cake!" he says.

"My, that's the funniest cake I've ever seen," says Sergeant Murphy, "but won't it taste good!"